HELEN OXENBURY
Pig Tale

Margaret K. McElderry Books
NEW YORK   LONDON   TORONTO   SYDNEY

Margaret K. McElderry Books
An imprint of Simon & Schuster Children's Publishing Division
1230 Avenue of the Americas, New York, New York 10020
Copyright © 1973, 2004 by Helen Oxenbury
Copyright renewed © 2001 by Helen Oxenbury
First published in Great Britain in 1973 by William Heinemann Ltd.
This U.S. edition, 2005
Published by arrangement with Egmont Books Limited
All rights reserved, including the right of reproduction in whole or in part in any form.
The text for this book is set in Bembo.
The illustrations for this book are rendered in gouache, pencil, and ink.
Manufactured in Italy
2 4 6 8 10 9 7 5 3
CIP data for this book is available from the Library of Congress.
ISBN 1-4169-0277-5

This is the story of two bored pigs.
She was called Bertha and his name was Briggs.
They would lie in the grass and moan and complain:
"Nothing happens to us—every day is the same!"

They had plenty to eat,   a warm sty with a thatch,

an orchard to play in   and trees for a scratch,

cool mud for a wallow,

fields full of flowers,

soft grass for a doze

or to gossip for hours.

But Bertha and Briggs were never content.
On money and riches their two minds were bent.
There were so many wonderful things they would do—
only then would they really be happy, they knew.

Then one sunny day they were nosing about,
when Briggs grubbed up a chest with the end of his snout.
They opened the lid with a squeal of delight,
for the chest contained treasure, all glittering bright.

"We are rich!" they cried out as they cleaned themselves down,
and clutching the chest, they set off for the town.

The noise of the traffic alarmed the two pigs,
and Bertha clung tight to the trotter of Briggs.

Briggs was soon dreaming of shiny new cars,
while Bertha gazed into shop windows for hours.

They came to a bank and looked shyly about
till the manager angrily ordered them out.

He ordered them out—then he noticed the box,
and his eyes had a gleam like a wily old fox.
Briggs lifted the lid of the treasure so rare—
the manager gasped and said, "Well, I declare!"
He bowed and he scraped and he said with a purr:
"Won't you please take a seat now, dear Madam and Sir?
I will give you some cash, Mr. Briggs, if I may.
You will find it is simpler than jewels when you pay."
He locked up the treasure behind a steel door
and gave them a case stuffed with banknotes galore.
"Thank you, oh thank you!" said Bertha with glee.
"Come, Briggs, let us start on our great shopping spree."

They went to a large and luxurious store,
where Bertha bought dresses and hats by the score.

Briggs's turn was next, and he felt quite a swell—
he tried on four suits and they fit him quite well.

From the store to the showrooms was not very far,
so they hurried to buy an expensive new car.

"This model's the latest," the car salesman said.
"Then I'll have it!" cried Briggs, feeling light in the head.

In jumped the two pigs, and they sped on their way
to purchase a house by the end of the day.

They went to an agent, who handed to Briggs
some pictures of houses just right for two pigs.

Bertha soon spotted the house with most charm—
the one she had seen from the gate on the farm.

The agent escorted them both to the door,
then left them alone to go in and explore.

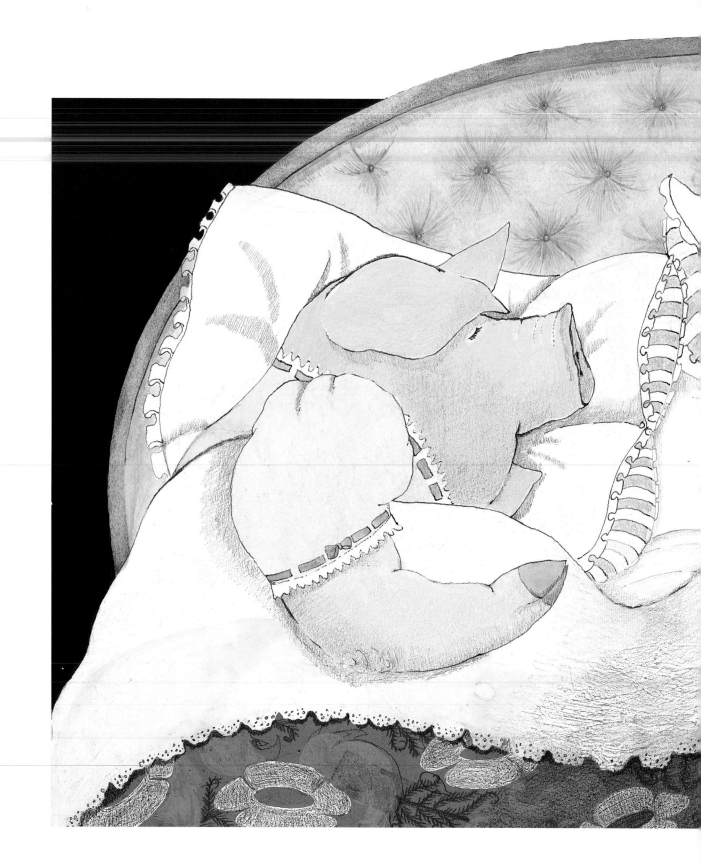

That night they were happy as two pigs could be,
and they talked and they planned until well after three.

But tossing and turning 'twixt blankets and sheet,
poor Briggs hardly slept on account of the heat.

Bertha made breakfast,   Briggs puttered about.

He polished the car,   she cleaned the house out.

Bertha cooked dinner while Briggs sat and read.

He made a few phone calls, they watched TV till bed.

One day, feeling restless with nothing to do,
while Bertha was busy preparing a stew,
Briggs drove his new car through the green countryside,
speeding down lanes that were not very wide.
Suddenly out of the engine there shot
a cloud of black smoke, and of steam boiling hot.
The car gave a cough and a lurch and a leap,
then rolled to a halt near a flock of white sheep.
Briggs lifted the hood and prodded around,
but the cause of the trouble just could not be found.
The longer he struggled, the madder he got,
till at last, in despair, very tired and too hot,
he threw down the wrench and uttered a moan—
he'd just have to start on the long walk back home.

When he opened the door, Briggs instantly knew
that Bertha's new gadgets were troublesome too.

"Oh Briggs," Bertha sobbed, "what a miserable day!
I've been working so hard, I've had no time to play."

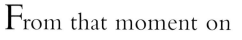

From that moment on   nothing seemed to go right.

House, garden, and pigs   were a terrible sight.

At last the two pigs   couldn't stand any more.

Briggs grabbed Bertha's arm,
and they dashed through the door.

From the garden they gazed at the country beyond,
and Briggs in a rage pushed his car in the pond.
They felt no regrets as they ran through the gate
and away from the life they had soon grown to hate.
They pulled off their clothes and ran on faster still—

didn't even look back as they tore up the hill.
Breathless, they ran through the old orchard gate—
for a roll in the mud the two pigs couldn't wait.
To be careless and free and to romp and to play
was all that they wanted to do every day.

That night as they lay gazing up at the sky,
Bertha and Briggs heaved a rapturous sigh.
"Let's stay here forever," said Bertha to Briggs,
and they fell fast asleep—two tired, happy pigs.

-4324